Cat and the Mail Truck

Written by Josh Rachford

Illustrated by Farwa Khan

To Forest, who loves mail trucks and cats

Cat and the Mail Truck
Published by Acer Lane Press
Manassas, Virginia

Library of Congress Cataloging-in-Publication Data

Rachford, Josh, 1985 –
    Cat and the Mail Truck
ISBN (hardcover): 9798986808208
ISBN (e-book): 9798976808215
LCCN: 2022916954

Acer Lane Ventures, LLC dba Acer Lane Press

A gray cat perched by his window each day
To see everything that came by that way.

A girl walked by with her dog in tow.
The dog said "woof!" so the cat meowed "hello!"

"Vroom!" A car raced down the street!

said the cat as he
stretched his feet.

hen all of a sudden -- what fabulous luck --
Came the cat's favorite thing:
the white mail truck!

Once every day that truck would come by
dropping off letters, and the cat wondered: why?

The driver walked up to the door with a box
and startled the cat with three loud KNOCKS!

The door opened up, the cat saw with glee.
With two jumps and a run the cat was now free!

He leapt up in the truck with a flick of his tail
and saw that the truck was all full of mail.

Meow!" said the cat to each box and each letter.
le said "meow!" again, the more times the better.

But then -- something moved! The cat thought "oh no!"
The driver was back, and the truck started to go.

The cat's little house looked smaller and smaller.
The cat felt quite scared and he started to holler.

"What's this?" said the driver. "A stowaway kitty?"
The cat cried, "meow!" and the postwoman felt pity.

"My mission," she said, "is taking things
where they go.
Come night or day, rain, sleet, or snow."

"Everything here has its place written **down**.

Its address describes where it goes in our **town**."

But the cat didn't know his home address,
"Meow meow meow meow," he had to confess.
"Poor little cat, I know what we'll do,

we'll go house to house and I'll show them to you.
When we come to your place, you'll let me know:
that's when you'll give out a great big MEOW."

They went down the road and in cul-de-sacs.
None were his home; the cat could not relax.

They stopped at apartments, houses, and shops;
The postwoman delivered at each of her stops.

As she returned to the truck the little cat saw
Sometimes she carried new mail in her paw

Just like the letters they delivered today
But with new addresses that could be far away

And right then and there the cat figured out
This was the reason the truck had its route!
ew things had to go to their places each day.The truck helped those
things along their way.

Then they rounded a corner and there the house stood: the cat's own little house in his own neighborhood.

"Meowl!" the cat said and the truck came to a stop.
With a purr as his thanks, he left with a hop.

At the door the cat meowed "Please let me in!"
The door opened up with a "Where have you been!?"

From that day on the cat stayed inside
but looked at the mail truck with a
feeling of pride.